JADV-PIC BLE
Henry! You're late again!
Bleckwehl, Mary Evanson
921207

# Henry!
## You're late AGAIN!

Written By
**Mary Evanson Bleckwehl**

Illustrations by
**Brian Barber**

This Book Belongs to _____

For my sister Nancy.
– MEB

For Aden and Wyatt.
– BB

ISBN 13: 978-1-59298-357-5

Library of Congress Catalog Number: 2010912891
Printed in the United States of America
First Printing: 2011
15    14   13   12   11        5   4   3   2   1

Cover and interior design by Brian Barber
Edited by Kellie Hultgren

BEAVER'S POND
PRESS

Beaver's Pond Press, Inc.
7104 Ohms Lane, Suite 101
Edina, MN 55439-2129
(952) 829-8818
www.BeaversPondPress.com

To order, visit www.BeaversPondBooks.com or call 1-800-901-3480. Reseller discounts available.
For more information visit www.marybleckwehl.com

**Today is Monday,**
and it's just another crazy morning at our house. I better hurry so I'm not late for school again. But what's the use?

Dad overslept.

I know what will happen if I arrive at school late again. I can just see tall Miss Timberlane, the school secretary, looking down her nose at me. Her irritated voice will rumble,

**"Henry! You're late AGAIN!"**

I wonder if **HER** father ever oversleeps.

Mom forgot to set the alarm clock Gramma gave her for Christmas.

# AGAIN!

I wonder if Miss Timberlane forgets to set her alarm clock. She probably has someone important, like the principal, give her a wake-up call each morning. They did that in the hotel last summer, the one we stayed in when Dad couldn't find our campground.

My sister, Isabela, can't find her polka-dotted socks—the ones that match her polka-dotted underwear. **AGAIN!**

Miss Timberlane probably doesn't wear socks. Maybe she doesn't even have feet. I can't tell because she's always behind that enormous brown desk in our school office.

My baby brother, Ryan, needs his diaper changed. **AGAIN!**

Do you think Miss Timberlane owns
a baby? She doesn't look like the
type who would put up with diapers,
if you know what I mean.

The zipper
on my new
jacket just broke.
Hmmmm…now that's never
happened before.

I doubt Miss Timberlane has a jacket. I've
never seen her wear one. In fact, I've never seen
her leave that desk to go anywhere! If she did, she
might miss something important—
like me coming in late AGAIN!

Besides, Miss Timberlane doesn't need a jacket. She lives at school.
At least that's what Sophie Hendricksen told me, and she's in second grade.

Maybe if I lived at school I would never be late.
I'll have to discuss this with Mom and Dad tonight.

I find my old jacket that I wore in kindergarten.
Finally I am ready to go to school.

Dad drives me the nine blocks.

"Hey, Henry! Look! No car line today!" Dad says.

He starts to whistle. He is obviously happy that the usual mile-long line of cars in front of South View Elementary School has disappeared.
I am thinking, "Yeah, that's because I'm REALLY late this time, and all the other kids are already at their desks."

Miss Timberlane isn't going to be happy. I'm doomed.

Dad drops me off near the front door of my school, and I shuffle to the office for my late slip.

Using my big muscles to heave the office door open, I nervously glance toward the secretary's desk.

There she is.

MISS TIMBERLANE.

But you'll never believe it! Miss Timberlane isn't looking down her nose at me. She isn't growling her usual "Henry! You're late AGAIN!" at me.

In fact, she is smiling! **At me!** She must be sick.

I mumble that I need a late slip, and she smiles some more. Maybe this is just someone disguised as Miss Timberlane. I study her closely to see if I can tell who the imposter is. I've seen this kind of thing on TV, where a bad guy pretends he's someone else. But this person doesn't look like a bad guy.

Her hair does look a bit different, and she's wearing an old sweatshirt that says **GO TIGERS** instead of her usual fancy clothes.

Then she speaks. But there's no grumbling. She sounds...well... downright nice!

**"No, Henry, you don't need a late slip.
Today is a teacher workday, and there is no school for students."**

And she smiles again, like she just gave me the Student of the Year gold medal.

# What? No school today?

Can I trust Miss Timberlane? **Or whoever this is?**

The gears in my head are turning.

Wait a minute. If there's no school, then what is Miss Timberlane doing here? Secretaries don't have to be here on TEACHER workdays, right?

I stare at her with my superspy eyes. **Ah HA!** I get it...I think Sophie Hendricksen is right! Miss Timberlane just MIGHT live at school. I peer around the room, looking for clues. I stare at Miss Timberlane's desk. I notice the steaming coffee mug. Right beside it is a plate with a frosted cinnamon roll and an orange—breakfast-like food! And is that an alarm clock sitting by her phone?

I smile at Miss Timberlane for the first time all year. I'm dying to ask her where she sleeps and where she hangs her jammies— maybe in the nurse's office.

NURSE'S OFFICE

Miss Timberlane calls my mom. "Your mother will be here in about an hour to pick you up, Henry."

## An hour?! What am I going to do until then?

Miss Timberlane moves out from behind her desk.

## Hey! She DOES have feet! And are those polka-dotted socks?!

"Henry, I have a problem I'm hoping you can help me with. Tomorrow morning the principal is going to be gone, so there's no one to read the morning announcements. I hear you are a terrific reader. Would you like to be the first student at South View to help me read the announcements over the loudspeaker?"

"Oh! That would be sweet!" I shout.

"Okay, then," Miss Timberlane says. "We have time to practice while you wait for your mom."

She leads me into the principal's office and tells me I can hop into his chair. I sit near the microphone. I can't believe this!

"Do you know what the principal likes to do more than anything else?" asks Miss Timberlane. I have **NO** clue.

"He likes to twirl in this chair."

"Twirl? No way!" I say.

"Yes, like this." Miss Timberlane twirls me around four times.

# Whoa!

Maybe I will be a principal someday and spend the day twirling and reading announcements.

We practice reading the announcements over and over. I read the birthdays, the newest books in the library, the lunch menu, and a good joke. And then I read the word of the day. Miss Timberlane reminds me to read this part slowly.

"The word of the day is '**patient**.' It means to wait calmly for something without complaining." I stop and ask, "What does THAT mean?"

Miss Timberlane thinks for a second. "Henry, there are times when you have to be patient and wait for others. You don't like being late, but getting angry doesn't solve your problem. Being patient makes it easier to make it a happy day even when you're late."

Uh-oh. That reminds me of something. Softly, I say, "Miss Timberlane, I hardly ever make it to school on time, and the announcements are read right away. I'm sorry, but if I'm late, I won't be able to help you read them, no matter how patient I am." And I stare at the floor.

"Would it help if I give your home
a wake-up call tomorrow?" she offers.

Before I answer,
I hear Mom's voice at the door.
"That would be perfect. And
the earlier, the better. We don't
want Henry to miss out on his
chance to help you."

"I'll see you tomorrow morning then, Miss Timberlane." My voice sounds happy and smart, and I smile real big at her.

"Okay, Henry," laughs Miss Timberlane. "Would you like me to give you a wake-up call EVERY morning?"

"Sure!" I say.

**"But not on teacher workdays."** And we all laugh.

As I turn to leave, I know exactly where I want to spend the rest of the day.

"Mom, can we check to see if I can play at Sophie's house this afternoon?"

"Sounds like a good plan, Henry," Mom says with a smile.

Sophie will want to hear ALL about the clues I discovered about Miss Timberlane. Maybe Sophie and I can become school spies together.

I think she's the smartest kid in school, next to me.